R.and S.

Christmas Carols

R.and S.

Christmas Carols

ISBN/EAN: 9783743420779

Manufactured in Europe, USA, Canada, Australia, Japa

Cover: Foto ©Andreas Hilbeck / pixelio.de

Manufactured and distributed by brebook publishing software
(www.brebook.com)

R.and S.

Christmas Carols

CHRISTMAS CAROLS.

BY R. & S.

1860.

CHRISTMAS CAROLS.

Christmas chiming from the valley,
Christmas chiming from the mountain,
Echoing o'er the frozen fountain,
Through the verdant pine tree alley ;
CHRIST has come to us from Heaven,
GOD, His Son to man has given !
    Christe Eleyson !

Winter Hymn--Snow.

Snow is falling—wildly falling—
In a gay fantastic round,
O'er the icy frozen ground,
Swiftly flying thro' the air;
 Whirl-winds floating, flying, racing,
 Eddies floating, flying, chasing,
Through the frosty, misty air.
 Every hill in white arrayed,
 Every tree in white arrayed,
'Tis as if the world had prayed
To put on mourning in that season,
For that short and hallow'd season,
 Ere the old year passed away.
Floweth on the tide of battle
 Of the elements of the sky;
From the loud and fiery rattle,
Of the fierce and angry battle,

To a faint and heaving sigh,
Of the elements of the sky.

Snow is falling—gently falling—
Thro' the icy breath of night;
Covering mounds up in the grave-yard,
Covering tombs up in the church-yard
    To the traveller a safeguard—
    If there be one out to-night.
Snow is falling on the dwelling
    Where the poor and good abide,
Falling on the sin and sorrow,
Striving good and bad to hide.
    Still it falls unceasingly;
Falling on the farmers cottage,
Maiden's youth, and old man's dotage;
    Still it falls unceasingly,
    Striving ever all to hide.

Snow is falling—gently falling—
    On the roof of rich and poor;
On the ancient time-worn castle
Shaking with its wintery moan
    Every casement with a rattle;
Still it falleth ever on!

6

Still it cometh ever down,
Covering even time's immortal
Echo of the distant portal,
  In the grey of Heaven's dome,
Still it cometh ever down.
Snow is falling on the ocean,
  On the cold and wintr'y ocean,
With a weary mournful motion;
And the storm—the wintr'y storm—
Wilh a wild and wailing shriek
From the mountains cragged peak
In a solemn icy column flows along;
Falling on the vessels deck,
Covering rope, and sail and spar,
Coming downward from afar
Thro' the cloudy, frosty night.
Falleth—falleth on forever;
  And the sailors on the sea,
While the snow falleth on
In its steady monotone
Pray to God—bend the knee
In the dread immensity
Of the cold—lone storm.

Snow is floating down from Heaven,

Resting on the lonely earth;
Winding 'neath the ancient pine trees,
'Neath the old and spreading lime trees,
   And the ancient sycamore,
   With a dull and distant roar.
Thro' the swelling of the storm,
Joyously is borne along,
   From the village in the valley,
   From the old bell in the valley,
A sweet and home-like chime;
   Rising in a cheerful echo,
Like some old and well known rhyme,
   From the old bell down below.
It is ringing in a blessing
   On the newly hallow'd earth;
On the heaving wind 'tis passing
   O'er the calmly sleeping earth,
With a hope of future cheer
To the young and new born year.

Snow is falling—gently falling—
   On the dark unbroken forest
   On the white and glittering hoar-frost,
On fountain and on rivulet
A graceful shadow seems to flit.

'Tis the snow—gentle snow—
With a white sepulchral flow,
Resting on the water fall,
Wreathing glories over all;
Still it falleth ever on !
Still it cometh ever down.
Snow is falling—gently falling—
   From the purple vaults of night,
   Gleaming with a silver light
In its soft and silent way,
   Peaceful as a child to slumber,
   Falling downward without number,
Rest the flakes so trustingly,
   In the enfolding arms of night;
Earth so sweetly gently holds them,
To her bosom now she folds them
   With a pressure—and a sigh
Seems to swell up from her bosom,
As a wail just passeth by;
   'Tis the sighing of the trees,
   'Tis the swaying of the trees,
   Of the old and solemn trees.

Snow is falling on the river—

On the dark and icy river—
  With a cold and death-like flow;
With a slow and mournful shiver,
  Heaving gently to and fro ;
Still it falls unceasingly !
  Still the symphony goes on !
'Tis the sighing of the branches,
As the ancient music launches
  Forth upon the sleeping earth;
Heaven's music riseth falleth,
Heaven's echo riseth falleth,
Heaven's angel gently calleth,
  In the tones of merry cheer;
'Tis the music of the storm,
As it gently flows along,
  'Tis the birth of the New-Year.

Snow is falling—gently falling—
  On the silent wearied city,
  Falling ever in its pity,
Striving ever all to hide.
  Still it falls unceasingly !
With its misty silent tide ;
With its white and flowing tide ;

Downward ever still 'tis falling,
  From the starless, murky, sky,
  Gently falleth, trustingly.

Falling on the good and bad,
On the happy and the sad,
On the fading and the dying,
On the hoping and the trying;
  Soothing every mortals sorrow,
  Making them forget the morrow.
Whiie the snow falleth on,
In its joyous baritone
  On the mourning and the weary,
  Driving from it all the dreary,
  Dreary grief with its gentle gentle flow.

Snow is falling—slowly, lightly—
And the New-Year's day is dawning !
In the east there comes the morning,
Welcoming in the New-Year's day.
Snow is falling, flake by fiake,
  As the morning's light is seen,
  And the day begins to break
  O'er the glad and cheerful scene;
  O'er the shining silver sheen

11

Of the wavy fallen snow,
And a voice to Heaven ascends—
To the Father's throne it wends
    Its way in trustfulness—
Asking for this New-Year
Nothing but hope and cheer,
Nothing of doubt and fear,
    But all of happiness.

The fire has gone out.

How cold it is in the sitting room !
A feeling of cheerlessness and gloom,
A wish for the warm air over all,
It shades the house like a gloomy pall;
It drives the blood from my heart away,
It makes my lips grow cold as clay;
There's a tinge of blue upon fingers and face,
For the fire's gone out in the chimney place.

The sorrows of years have come to me,
As the hoar-frost rocks the gigantic tree,
The age of love and hope and pride,
The age of longing and faith has died,
And I look up to the light on high,
Every hour it draweth nigh,
The light and beauty has left my face,
For the fire is out in the chimney place.

I am so weary of earthly ills,
Weary of earth rising sickening chills,
Of the care, the sorrow, that I must bear,
Weary of life and life's dull care;

13

Weary of meeting day after day
The same heart-burnings every way;
Weary of seeing the wheat and tare
Choking each other every where.

And I've no home to receive me now,
No gentle hand to caress my brow;
The shades of death have darkened it,
The ravens upon its rafters sit;—
And the wind moans drearily thro' the door,
Where I shall be greeted; oh, nevermore—
And life is gone, 'tis sad, sad truth
The fire is out in the home of my youth;

And I wait in grief the sad year thro',
Striving to do the right and true,
Striving to conquer the dull despair
That is eating out my heart with care,
Striving to stay the murmur at fate,
Striving to enter the narrow gate,
Striving to feel that I'm not alone;
But the fire is out in my heart of stone.

Now a light breaks thro' the shades of life,
A parting of all the elements of strife,

14

A trust in God and a hope in him,
A lightening of vapor once so dim,
A trial between my guardian fays—
Wishes for brighter and happier days—
A release from sorrow and grief and pain;
For the light of hope is rekindled again.

Now and Then.

Two lovers stood by the side of a stream,
Dreaming together Love's sweet dream;
    Hand in hand alone;
Love's sweet music—wondrous and rare—
In rich cadences was filling the air,
    And the brook flowed on.

Listening unto the streamlets flow,
An old man stands with locks of snow;
    Silent and weary and lone;
Silent and weary with drooping head,
While still in its moss grown pebbly bed
    The brook flowed on.

Stanzas.

—

"Tis but a question of time;
A year or two—no more—
Never a sea or clime,
Or medicine's mighty lore,
Can keep me now to thee;
Never a feeling of pain,
Or of sorrow comes to me,
For I will come home again.

'Tis but a question of time,
Never a thought of sorrow,
The love and the faith are mine—
It may be even to-morrow.
A few years now at the best,
Beloved we shall be parted,
I shall go gently to rest;
And you will stay broken hearted.

'Tis but a question of time;
One of God's grain needs reaping,
Near the eleventh hour;
But why should ye be weeping.

Soon away I am going,—
Without any hardship or pain—
The reaping must follow the sowing—
But I will come home again.

To a Bird.

The fields are covered with snow, little bird,
    And chill is the wintry air;
The brook is still in its icy sheath,
    And the trees are stark and bare.

The flowers, the fair bright flowers, little bird,
    Withered and dark are they,
Faded their beauty with summers last smile,
    And their fragrance hath long passed away.

Fly back to the sunnier land, little bird,
    And when the bright summer shall come,
When flowers are blooming in natures glad smile,
    Return to your northern home.

Occasio,

When God in his etherial wisdom,
Made the world—he did create it all
One Summer—and when Adam came
He found the earth a tedious monotone of smiles;
The sky, and air, and every living thing
Was scorched with heat—the mighty sea
Upon the unworn rocks combed up
Its moulten surf—the very deep did seem
A well of lava—e'en the blood of nature,
As it flowed o'er beds of gold, a sapphire stream —
Smoked hot and heavy as a flesh pot;
But, in the garden where dwelt Adam,
Lock'd by rivers which did flow from hills
Of ice beyond—eternal freshness reigned;
Not the hot breathing of the forest isles
Were wafted there—but life was all repose,
And love, and beauty;—all was fresh and still
In Eden.
Now the days and years swept by—and year by year
A change came oe'r the world—the cold crept in
Her habitations, and the autumn came,
And buds did fade and wither, but the forest grew

18

More beauteous still.—'Twas summer still in Eden ;
In its paradise the red grape grew ripened,
And fruits gave unto Adam of their increase.
O'er all the beauty of God reigned—
His image stamped upon the face of nature—
His glory pictured in his handiwork.
Then the temptation came, and then the fall;
Adam was banished from the garden,
And the angel with the flaming sword,
Stood at the portal.—Eden is his no more ;
For the great wrath of God o'ershadowed all
And the dread cold grew daily more and more;—
Then the frail covering of figs did not suffice
To keep the gloom and darkness from his soul;
Then winter came, and chill and ice
Reigned o'er the unhappy world—
And disobedience was punished—but at last
The all-wise God relented and forgave the sin of Adam;
And the sun rose up once more in splendor,
And the sky softened her tints in beauty.
The broad earth grew beautiful again.
Then spring-time came—a mighty voice
Did whisper to each tree and vine,
Arise shake off thy robe of cold
19

And live again.   The flowers grew forth,
And leaves and plants burst their ice mantle,
And light shone like a new glory thro' the sky
The great God was gloried in his glorious work,
And thro' the world their sped
From every living thing a voice of praise—
The earth itself grew young and chanted forth
Its thankfulness for this great blessing—
For life's fittest season—spring.

Thoughts at Christmas.

Before the fire I sit to day,
And muse on scenes that long have flown,
And friends that from my side have gone;
The scenes are lifeless—friends are clay.

At Christmas tide a merry throng
Were wont to gather round this hearth,
With sounds of revelry and mirth,
And joyous hearts and gleeful song.

But they are all forever gone;
A few slight traces still remain,
Like the last half-mown spears of grain
In a large cheerless field alone.

Only a few stray locks of hair,
Long severed from reposing heads;
Some interspersed with silver threads,
And some are radiant and fair.

The voices that like music gushed,
The radiant cheeks, the laughing eyes,

Each treasure in the dim past lies;
Their light is fled their music hushed.

The grass has grown and faded oft
Since their warm grasp has met my own,
Yet still I seem to hear the tone,
Of merry voices sounding soft.

And oftentimes I start with pain,
As walking in the crowded street,
A glance persuades me that I meet
Some cherished friend of youth again.

I weep as one by one to mind,
Their faces sadly I recall,
As memory lifts the sable pall
From the dim vista far behind.

Earnest and long on me they gaze,
With tearful and imploring eyes
As if they wished me to arise
And join their pleasant quiet ways.

From all the trouble and the strife,
The weary pain, the weary woe,

I constant meet where'er I go
Upon the long dark road of Life,

They seem my willing soul to draw
From this cold earth with all its care,
Their sweet society to share,
Upon Eternity's far shore.

Frozen to Death.

She has walked the whole of the livelong day
To look for food for her orphan child,
And her heart grows faint and her eye grows wild
As the night comes on and her steps gives way.

The stars are out in the clear blue sky;
Oft she has watched them shining there,
When her step was light and her cheek was fair
In the pleasant years that have long gone by.

She has blessed them a thousand times and now
She will not curse them were she to die;
And her bosom heaves with a bursting sigh,
And a moment with fire is flushed her brow.

Press on, press on, nor stop to recall
Those scenes of Joy to life and light,
The present and future are dark as night,
But the past is darker far than all.

She presses her babe to her shivering breast,
And holds him there in a mute embrace;

24

Her wan hands cover his pale cold face,
And she knows he has fled to a sweeter rest.

Fallen ! They have fallen to earth at last !
Mother and child to the pavement cold;
And the midnight chime their knell hath tolled;
Misery, Dearth and Hunger are past.

The rough winds played with her flowing hair,
And the morning rose with a cloudless sky,
And the passer shuddered as hurrying by
He saw the form as it stiffened there.

Cold and motionless, void of breath,
There they lay in a last embrace,
Bosom to bosom and face to face,
Frozen to Death ! Frozen to Death !

Thanksgiving Hymn.

Glory to God on this our Thanksgiving,
Glory to God for his wonderful name,
Glory to God for his wonderful giving,
For the light and the love and the sun and the rain.
We worship with honest hearts deepest devotion,
Praising for gifts of his might all sublime;
Praise with a nations most fervent emotion
For gifts he will send to the ending of time.

Glory to God on this our thanksgiving,
Glory to God for this plenteous year;
He that hath guarded us in his great given,
Still He will keep us from doubt and from fear.
Rising of tempests may battle around us,
Nations may war with unhallow'd creed;
He who in danger and misery found us
He will be with us in every hearts need.

Glory to God on this our thanksgiving,
To the worker of all—in all marvelous ways;

26

Homage to Him be ye reverent giving,
Homage to him as a nations fond praise.
Give God the praise to him only 'tis due,
We are treading a narrow and treacherous road;
For all he has done unto me and to you
Lighten the weight of some sufferer's load.

Glory to God on this our thanksgiving,
Glory for all the kind deeds he has done,
Thou dost not see all, oh, thou unbelieving
Do these blessings not brighten one after one.
One after one, with constant endevour,
God calleth back his own erring child;
Strange that a mortal should try to dissever
This love from our paradise once so defiled.

Glory to God on this our thanksgiving,
He has been with us the long long year thro',
Pray in the depths of our honest believing
He may be by us another year too!
Give God the Glory—-be ever addressing
The source of all good—the great Fatl er sublime!
Upon that dear faith will we ever be resting,
'Till we are no more—at the ending of time.

Song.

Far away in a distant clime
Where the vines o'er the hills are creeping,
Where the golden sunlight purples the grape,
The fairest of maids lies sleeping.
Cruel fate tore her away from my side,
When the star of hope grew brightest,
Sorrow came brooding gloomy and black
Like a cloud, when my heart was lightest.

Why do I mourn ? There's a brighter land
Where the fairest of beings are dwelling;
She is there looking down with her old sweet smile
And her happiness seems to be telling.
I go ; to leave the world with its cares,
Its wretchedness and its sorrow,
I go to be clasped in a fond embrace,
And awake to a glad to-morrow.

28

Pax Illiscum.

A monarch is laying him down to die,
　From his careworn brow he lifts his crown,
And without a murmur, without a sigh,
　He lays the regal bauble down.

Weary of Life and longing for Death,
　Heavily on his couch he lies,
Wearily comes his wasting breath—
　Closing fast are his languid eyes.

In the vacant streets lies the virgin snow,
　And the city is lost in a tranquil sleep,
And naught but the river's distant flow
　Is heard as it surges mighty and deep.

Would our hearts if we asked them, long to be
　Where He passeth lonely away to-night,
On the silent shore of the mystic sea,
　Afar from sorrow and care and blight?

29

Hark ! The midnight chime begins,
  On the night the echoes swell—
Christ forgive us all our sins—
  'Tis the old year's funeral knell.

A spirit floats out on the night,
  With wan hands crossed on a shrouded breast,
Silent and spectral, still and white,—
  Trouble it not—it is going to rest.

Monks are passing along below,
  Hooded and dark with solemn tread;
Chaunting an anthem weird and slow;
  Chaunting an anthem for the dead.

Pax illiscum; rest his soul;
  He at last has reached his goal,
On that distant unknown shore,
  Pax illiscum; evermore.

Distant music is heard afar
  Swelling in symphonies deep and grand,
A royal infant crowned with a star,
  Heads a radiant shining band.

Lo! From the deep unknown there springs,
  Time's latest off-spring the Young New-Year;
A laughing child with lightsome wings,
  And he crosses himself o'er the old man's bier.

Soft are the echoes that die away;
  Sweet are the strains that swell afar;
Brightly amid the dim clouds grey,
  Shineth the glory of yonder star.

Come, O, my friends, the night wanes fast,
  And the New-Year shines o'er fields of snow;
And over the dreary drifts of the past,
  Hope sheds a radiant heavenly glow.

November.

How desolate the moorland lies !
The tall trees waving in the skies,
Shorn of their leafy covering ;
While above the grey gull hovering,
Screaming forth dull notes of pain,
Which dying out, in echo comes again.
The buisy tramp of men is gone;
The earth seems desolate and lone.
The dull deep roar of the appealing woods
Fills all—into our heart intrudes
Its dull inanity: and frozen all,
Locked up in death's embrace, a pall
Rests on the world;—ice is a dreary thing,
I pray to God the advent of the spring !

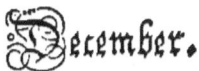December.

Golden-haired autumn has fled at thy coming!
Skies blush with kisses the sun gives no more,
The song of the robin the wood-peckers druming,
Comes faintly and low from the warm southern shore.

The call of the sea bird, the gull and the swallow,
The voice of the bittern, the cry of the mew
Are echoing harshly, so dreary and hollow,
From the vale and the woodland and sea-meadow too.

The dark ocean rocks with its limitless roar;
They spray flings aloof its grey misty foam;
And thro' the thick fog that lies skirting the shore,
The curleu shrieks forth its wild wearisome tone.

The flight of the eagle is low, and his young
Are seized by the wolf in his ravenous prowl;
The voice of the day is stilled, hushed is its song;—
And the voice of night is the screach of the owl.

Blithe-crested autumn has fled at thy coming!
Skies blush with kisses the sun gives no more,
Dark and desponding, December is coming—
The days of the dying the tomb of the year.

nward.

Onward fly onward oh time in your track,
In the race never falter or doubting look back,
Let me never remember the days that are past,—
On, onward with beating heart onward and fast !
The tear of deep sorrow, the penitant prayer,
The sigh of the stricken of heart broken care,
Hide all from me while I strive of the track,
And oh, may I never with faint heart look back !

Oh vanish the past let the future abide,
Tho' we know not what evil or good may betide,
Where the grand voices echo from realms all unknown
To the chant of the pilgrim in silvery tone.
On, onward and upward with counsel within,
Life has her triumphs for those who will win ;
Onward fly onward oh time on thy track
In the race never falter or doubting look back.

Oh visions of wisdom—the cheek of the seer
Glows with proud pity his eye with a tear—

In halos of glory the future shines forth,
As the lightnings of heaven gleam out in the North,
He sees in the distance the grandner to come,
'Tis the shadows of Heaven that long-hoped for home,
Oh beckon me on while I strive on the track—
And oh may I never with faint heart look back.

Oh never look back for the *present* is fair,
Fairer than aught that the future can bear,
Oh, joy be to us that we live in a day
When the past and its missions vanish away ;
When the light of great reason from spiritful lands,
Is weaving earth glories with mystical hands ;
Oh joy be to us that we dwell in a realm
With angels for counsel and Faith at the helm.

Oh never look back the present is rife,
With all that maketh as happy in life,
The past is all sealed and faided and dead—
She has faded away in her snow covered bed ;
And the light of the sun with its mystlcal ray
Shines down from her hight in a becoming way,
It calleth us on to the end—calleth on—
Till we reach wan and weary the long hoped for bourne.

Retrospective.

In the splendor of the Autumn, neath a giant beech and
    olden, *beloved,*
When the forest leaves are turning dusky, red and golden.

At our feet the babbling streamlet ever murmured forth
    its story,
Told of noble deeds and worthy, love, and fame and glory.

And the oak tree tall and stately, and the elm tree gent-
    ly swaying,
And the willow softly sweeping, heard what we were
    saying.

Words of love fell soft as music, and the streamlet bub-
    bling proudly,
Told the tale to rock and lillies,—told the story proudly.—

Thou art mine, mine own, my beauty, thou art mine for-
    ever,
And the strong love-tie that binds us nought   but death
    can sever.

Streams have scarred the ancient oak tree, snows have
    blighted the wild heather,

36

Ice has bound the merry streamlet were we sat together.

As the dreary Autumn twilight scenes that long ago I
    cherished,
Rise before me still and ghostly—but their their light
has perished.

Voices in the air around me whisper with the trees low
    sighing,
And the dead leaves slowly falling with the Autumn dy-
    ing.

I've heard them, often heard them, but one voice my soul
    has haunted,
Rising clear above the others—one sad song is chaunted.

Leaves have fallen—winds are wailing, o'er the hill-side
    and the meadow,
Falls the sable pall of winter, light gives place to shadow.

Labor is Honor.

Labor is honor and worship thanksgiving !
  Glory to God for his wonderful name,
Glory to God for his wonderful giving,
  For the light, and the love, and the sun, and the rain.
Thro' fairy chancels of oak leaf and clover,
  God with his mystic voice whispers divine ;
The dew and the sunshine the mighty world over
  Are given to labor—the fruit of the vine.

Labor is honor and praise, adoration !
  Glory to God for the days that are gone ;
Labor for him 'tis a wide world's libation,—
  Labor to sever the fig from the thorn.
Thro' aisles of story in barberous ages,
  Shrine of the great and the lost we deplore,
Read of the past in the marvellous pages—
  Of history—the light and the reasons of lore.

Labor is honor—the good that thou doeth !
  Shall be a libation to heavenly love ;
The wounds that thou healeth, the seed that thou soweth
  Shall all be a recompense for thee above.

'Tis not the labor that honors thy dwelling,
  'Tis but the spirit thou doest it in,—
Angels are harking—ye earth's mission telling,
  The secrets of life in thy warm heart within.

Labor is honor—the corn-field and meadow
  Echo God's praise from the bountiful shore ;
Labor has kept from our homes the dark shadow ;
  Labor is keeping the wolf from the door.
Labor is ever unchanging unceasing
  Giving to God the just praise that is due,
From sorrow and care it is ever releasing ;
  Labor is happy for labor is true.

Labor is honor—the soul of a mortal
  Striving with demons the hold of his own ;—
Up the dark road and to enter the portal,
  Ahead of his fellows to enter alone.
Commerce and art with their kindred relations ;
  The labor of heart and the trumpth of mind,
The praise of a few, the rejoicing of nations ;
  The love and the honor each good of its kind.

Labor is honor—the fettered and freeman
  Knoweth its value more priceless than gold ;

Labor is honor the landsman and seaman
    Lesteth wherever lifes story is told.—
Labor is hallow'd the good God has told us,
    From the sinning of Adam of old until now,
That the bonds of steam labor must ever enfold us ;
    "Bread shall thou eat by the sweat of thy brow."

Song of the Moon.

Brightly as onward I move,
Falls on the Castle's wall my light,
Falls on the cottage thatch as bright,
    Soft as the smile of love.

Resteth my blessing on all,
Far over meadow and woodland and sea,
Beggar and prince are alike to me,
    Hovel and stately hall.

Centuries, ages roll on,
Still do I keep my radient way,
Casting on sorrow a cheering ray,
    When the hope of love is gone.

40

Faith.

Faith is trust ? a sturdy will,
  That will ever struggle on ;
Looking ever up the hill,
  Towards the ever distant bourne.

Faith is truth, no word of cavil
  Can its holy virtue check ;
Never heeding all life's evil,
  Through the storm of life's sad wreck.

Faith is love—a life's emotiom,
  Love of God and love to man,
Of an honest heart's devotion ;
  Who, through life does what he can.

Faith is hope, eternal sorrow,
  Ne'er can check it ne'er deplore ;
Looking ever to the morrow,
  Something better something more.

Faith is freedom tempered ever,
  By the world through which we go,
While we're passing down the river
  To the mystic vale below.

A Voice from the hills of Bethlehem.

Starry night is falling gently
  Over the hills of Bethlehem !
Angel voices whisper gently
  Over the hills of Bethlehem !
Mingling with the joyous murmur,
  Of the villages of Bethlehem;
    And the angel voices whisper,—
      Holy lay,
'Jesus our saviour's born to day !

Blessed Christmas night hallow'd thou'lt ever be!
  Upon the hills of Bethelem
We prayerfully bend the knee.
  Upon the hills of Bethlehem,
Man was redeemed by Thee.
  Blessed christmas night—voices still whisper;
      Gently say,
'Jesus our savior's born to-day !'

T'was on this night that long ago he came,
  Ou these dear hills of Bethlehem ;

There with his holy name
 Hallowed the hills of Bethlehem ;
The same as in the olden time.
 Stand those dear hills of Bethlehem ;
And as of old the voices whisper,—
   Holy lay,
'Jesus our saviour's born to-day !'

The Burden of a Sigh.

What a world of bitter waiting,
What a world of tender greeting,
   It could tell !

What prayer, and fear, and sorrow,
What longing for the morrow,
   It could tell !

What griefs, and hearts most broken,
What love and grief unspoken,
   It could tell !

What misery and wretchedness,
What longing for true blessedness,
      It could tell !

What triumph and what failing,
What brightening and what paling,
      It could tell !

What deep font of recollection
Beyond humanity's expression
      It could tell !

Of the long-forgotten pleasure,
Of the heart's securest treasure,
      It could tell !

44

A Merry Christmas and a Happy New-Year.

The icicles hang on the outer wall,
    And the wind mourns thro' the snow;
Within the light on the Christmas hall
    Lends to all a cheerful glow.
The poor ones cluster in the street,
    And look thro' the frosted pane,
A sight of splendor their visions greet
    As they never may see again.

CHORUS.

Now a blessing on all and a season of cheer;
Merry Christmas to all and a Happy New Year!

Let the poor enter for once to night,
    And sing in the Christmas hall,
Let us gather our brothers around the light
    Of the bright Christmas festival;
Join hands ye brothers—oh never grieve,
    Rejoice that a KING is born

This is our Holy Christmas eve,
   And to-morrow is Christmas morn !
     CHORUS—Now a blessing on all, &c.

Wave the holly round the hall,
   Let no man sorrow or grieve,
'Tis the night of the Christmas festival
   'Tis the Holy Christmas eve;
Join hands my brothers round the board,
   We will by the elfin's leave
Give to-night to the poor our hand,
 • On this Holy Christmas eve.

     CHORUS—Now a blessing on all, &c.

Sing of the glories of Christmas time;
   Oh friends the holly wave;
Do ye not hear the Christmas chime,
   On this our Christmas eve?
Sing merrily oh ye dancing light,
   Rejoice that a KING is born;
For this is our holy Christmas night,
   And to-morrow is Christmas morn !

     CHORUS—Now a blessing on all, &c.

Rejoice for some work that ye have done

46

'To allay some earthly sorrow,
For the path of duty once begun
    Will not be ended to-morrow.
And oh a shout at these merry days,
    The season of blithesome mirth,
The time of the year for household lays
    To be chanted over the earth.

     CHORUS—Now a blessing on all, &c.

Fill high my comrades chaunt aloof
    The lays of Christmas time,
Chaunt till over the chapels roof
    We hear the Christmas chime.
Then lower the bowl and bend the head,
    Bow to the Christ that's born,
Bow to the King in the manger bed,
    For to morrow is Christmas morn !

     CHORUS—Now a blessing on all, &c.

Good night to all dear friends, good night,—
    The moon is shining o'er the snow,
While thro' its gentle mellow light,
    A welcoming voice doth seem to flow:
Welcome the coming Christmas day,

Let never a mortal sorrow;
Chaunt a welcome and wreathe the bay,
And welcome the Christmas morrow.

CHORUS—Now a blessing on all, &c.

Good night—the echos die away,
The good men clasp each other's hands,
In a most reverent silent way
They praise the Savior of all lands.
They are not sad—they do not grieve;
In Judea a King is born,
For this is the holy Christmas eve,
And to-morrow is Christmas morn !

CHORUS.

Now a blessing on all and a season of cheer;
Merry Christmas to all and a Happy New-Year!

R. A. REED, PRINTER.

www.ingramcontent.com/pod-product-compliance
Lightning Source LLC
Chambersburg PA
CBHW022203020726
47496CB00008B/2848